GILBERT THE HERO

To Andrew and Robert, and brotherly love!
J.C.

For Fin
C.F.

The great white shark is one of the supreme predators of the ocean. White sharks can grow to about
6 meters, the females being a little bigger than the males, and can weigh over 3 tons. But, in spite of their size,
white sharks can leap clear out of the water!

White sharks are found in parts of the Pacific, Atlantic, and Indian Oceans, and in the Mediterranean Sea.
Because of their rarity and secretive behavior, there is much we do not know about great white sharks.

In warmer waters sharks are often accompanied by a small fish called a remora. Remoras can have
a close relationship with a shark, scavenging for leftover food and nibbling off shrimp-like parasites that grow
on the shark's body. The remora may stay with a single shark for a while, hitching a lift by sticking to the shark's
underside with a special sucker found on its head.

The Shark Trust is the conservation charity dedicated to the study, management, and conservation of sharks.
To find out more about sharks, become a member, or adopt a shark like Gilbert simply visit www.sharktrust.org.

STERLING and the distinctive Sterling logo are registered trademarks of Sterling Publishing Co., Inc.

Lot#:
2 4 6 8 10 9 7 5 3 1
09/10

Published in 2010 by Sterling Publishing Co., Inc.
387 Park Avenue South, New York, NY 10016
Text © 2010 by Jane Clarke
Illustrations © 2010 by Charles Fuge
Distributed in Canada by Sterling Publishing
c/o Canadian Manda Group, 165 Dufferin Street
Toronto, Ontario, Canada M6K 3H6

First published in Great Britain in 2010 by Simon and Schuster UK Ltd
1st Floor, 222 Gray's Inn Road, London, WC1X 8HB
A CBS Company

Printed in China
All rights reserved.

Sterling ISBN 978-1-4027-8040-0

For information about custom editions, special sales, premium and
corporate purchases, please contact Sterling Special Sales
Department at 800-805-5489 or specialsales@sterlingpublishing.com.

GILBERT THE HERO

by Jane Clarke
illustrated by Charles Fuge

STERLING

New York / London

"This is my little brother, Finn," Gilbert the great white shark proudly told his friend Rita Remora. "Mom says he can come to the park with us. We can teach him all our games."

"But he's too small to play with us," Rita grumbled. "He'll ruin everything."

"No, he won't," Gilbert grinned. "We'll have great fun together. Come on!"

Gilbert took Finn by the fin as they all swam off to the park.

"Don't let Finn out of your sight!"
Mrs. Munch called after them.

"Let's go on the sea-saw first," Gilbert said,
sitting Finn on the low end.
Rita sat with Finn to balance it.
"Hold tight!" she called, as Gilbert
hurled himself on the high end.

THUMP!

The sea-saw hit the sea bed.

WHEEE!

Finn and Rita catapulted out of the water, somersaulted through the air . . .

. . . and fell back into the ocean with a SPLASH!

"Waaah!" yelled Finn. "Waaah!"

"Finn's too small for this game," Rita told Gilbert.

"How about a game of finball?"

Gilbert placed an empty sea urchin in front of his little brother.
"Now whack it with your tail," he said.

Finn flapped his tail with all his might,

but he couldn't hit the urchin.

"Waaah!" he yelled. **"Waaah!"**

"Never mind," Gilbert told him.

"I'll flick it to you. You try to stop it."

"Be careful, Gilbert," called Rita.

But it was too late!

Gilbert flicked the urchin hard with his tail . . .

...THUNK!

The urchin hit Finn in the tummy.
"Waaah" he yelled, as he was
bowled over and over and over.
"Waaah!"

"Finn's too small for this game, too," said Rita.

"You're right," Gilbert sighed. "We can't play ANY of our old games with Finn."

"Cheer up," Rita said. "Let's put him on the seaweed swing while we think of something else."

Gilbert and Rita watched Finn
swing to and fro on the seaweed
swing at the edge of the park.
The little shark chuckled as a
school of silvery fish shimmered
around him.
"Finn's having fun now,"
Rita smiled.

"But it isn't very exciting, is it?"
Gilbert grumbled.
Just then, Marvin the Mallet
zoomed into the park on his skate.
"Now, that's what I call exciting!"
Gilbert said.

Marvin skidded to a halt in front of Gilbert
and Rita. "Want a turn?" he asked.
Gilbert's eyes lit up. "Yes, please!" he said.

"But what about Finn?" Rita asked.

"He'll be okay," said Gilbert. "We can keep an eye out for him."

Gilbert checked that his little brother was safely strapped in his swing.

"We won't be long," he told Finn.

Gilbert and Rita whizzed around
the park, waving at Finn every time
they passed the swing.

Finn giggled happily as they skated by.

But all of a sudden, the sea behind the
seaweed swing went as dark as night.
The school of fish scattered into
a shower of sparkles and an
enormous whale swept out
of the seaweed with a
beak full of fish.

A killer whale!

Gilbert was so shocked he fell off the skate!

"Waaah!" Finn yelled. "Waaah! Waaah!"

The whale's eyes widened as it spat
out its mouthful of tiny fish.

"Oh, no!" gasped Gilbert. "It's seen Finn!"
"And you strapped him in the swing!" Rita cried.
"Finn's trapped. That whale will eat him for lunch!"

"Not if I can help it!" said Gilbert, thrashing his tail with all his might. The water churned and foamed as he rocketed toward his little brother.

But would he get there in time?

The whale opened his jaws
just as Gilbert chomped
through the seaweed
swing and dragged
Finn away.

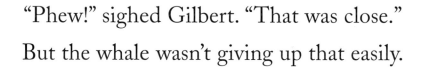

"Phew!" sighed Gilbert. "That was close."
But the whale wasn't giving up that easily.

"Look! It's coming back!"
cried Rita. "We have to
get out of here, Gilbert!"

"The Wreck!" Gilbert gasped. "We can hide in the Wreck!"

Gilbert and Rita swam frantically toward the Wreck, dragging Finn's swing between them. The whale's jaws snapped at their tails.

"Quick! Hide in here!"

Gilbert pushed Finn and Rita toward a small hole in the Wreck. He dived into the cabin. The sea swirled as the whale nosed around the Wreck. It was getting closer and closer to Gilbert's hiding place. Gilbert shuddered as an enormous black eye filled the cabin window. He held his breath.

THUNK! The whale's head stuck in the window frame.

CRAAACK!

The wood splintered as it backed away.

"You're too big to get us!" Gilbert grinned.

Then, with a flick of its tail, the whale was gone.

"You can come out now," Gilbert called to Rita and Finn.
"The whale is gone."
But there was no sign of Finn or Rita. Gilbert felt
his stomach sink. He frantically searched all the empty
hiding places. Had the whale eaten Finn and Rita?

"Boo!"

Finn and Rita popped out of a barrel on the sea bed.
"Aargh!" Gilbert yelled, leaping into the sea and flapping
his fins in surprise.

"Do it again!" chuckled Finn.

Rita giggled. "You were right, Gilbert" she said.
"It IS fun playing with Finn. And he's really good at ONE of our games . . ."

"Tide-and-seek!" Gilbert grinned.

$\mathcal{F}_{in}$